Topsy and Tim Visit London

By Jean and Gareth Adamson

Illustrations by Belinda Worsley

A catalogue record for this book is available from the British Library

Published by Ladybird Books Ltd
A Penguin Company
Penguin Books Ltd., 80 Strand, London WC2R 0RL, UK
Penguin Books Australia Ltd., 707 Collins Street, Melbourne, Victoria 3008, Australia
Penguin Group (NZ) 67 Apollo Drive, Rosedale, North Shore 0632, New Zealand

012

© Jean Adamson MMXII
Reissued MMXIV

ISBN: 978-1-40930-947-5
Printed in China

www.topsyandtim.com

It was Topsy and Tim's first visit to London.
They were staying in Boris's house. Boris was a big
ginger cat. He belonged to Mummy's best friend.

On Monday morning, Mummy and Dad took Topsy and Tim to
the Tower of London. They went there on a big red London bus.
"I can see the Tower!" said Mummy.
"It looks like a castle," said Topsy.
"I like castles," said Tim.

Soon they were inside the Tower's walls, watching
two knights in armour having a sword fight.
"I wish I had a sword," said Tim.

Topsy enjoyed watching a Beefeater feed the big, black ravens that live in the Tower of London. "As long as the ravens stay in the Tower, our kingdom will be safe," said the Beefeater to Topsy.

On Tuesday morning, Topsy and Tim went on a
London Underground train.
"Ooooer," said Topsy as they went down, down,
down on the escalator.

The underground train was noisy but fast. It was
taking them to see the changing of the guards at
Horse Guards Parade.

There were lots of horses at the parade, with soldiers riding them. The horses were beautiful and they were clever, too.

"I wish I could have a ride on a horse," said Topsy.

On Wednesday, Topsy and Tim went up the River Thames in a boat. They passed the London Eye. It was turning round very, very slowly, like a great big bicycle wheel.

A clock called Big Ben stood on the other side of the river.
It began to chime as they floated past.
"Bong-bong-bong, bong-bong-bong, bong-bong-bong,
BONG!" chimed the clock.
"That's ten o'clock," said Tim.

The boat chugged all the way up the river to Kew Gardens. Topsy and Tim raced about in the gardens and took Mummy and Dad high up on the Treetop Walkway.

Best of all was a hot, steamy jungle in a huge glass-house. Topsy thought she saw a monkey in a palm tree and Tim spotted a bunch of bananas.

IGUANODON

STEGOSAURUS

On Thursday morning, they went to see the dinosaurs in the Natural History Museum. Topsy and Tim loved the dinosaurs. The models looked almost real.

PSITTACOSAURUS

DINOSAUR EGGS

Some of the dinosaurs looked friendly, others looked rather fierce. They all had very long names.

"Look, said Dad. There's a Tyrannosaurus Rex."
The Tyrannosaurus Rex looked like a model, but suddenly
it turned its head, opened its mouth and ROARED.

Topsy and Tim were really scared!
"It's all right," said Mummy. "It's only a model."

On Friday morning, Dad took Topsy and Tim to
Diana's Playground in Kensington Gardens. There
were swings and slides to go on, teepees to play in,
pools to paddle in and lots of sand to dig in.

Best of all was a real pirate ship for children to
climb on and sail the stormy seas.
"I'm the queen of the pirates," shouted Topsy.
"And I'm the captain of the ship!" shouted Tim.

It was time to go back to Boris's house for tea.
On the way they stopped to look at a golden statue.
"Is it a statue or is it a man standing very still?" said Dad.

Topsy and Tim jumped when the statue suddenly smiled at them. It was a real man after all. Dad took a photograph of the golden man to show Mummy.

On Saturday, it was time for Topsy and Tim and Mummy and Dad to go home. Saying goodbye to Boris was sad, but it was great to see their own dear Kitty again.

Now turn the page and help
Topsy and Tim solve a puzzle.

Topsy and Tim had a fantastic time on their visit to London.
Here are some of the things they saw. Can you look back
through the book and remember where they saw each one?

KITTY ROSE

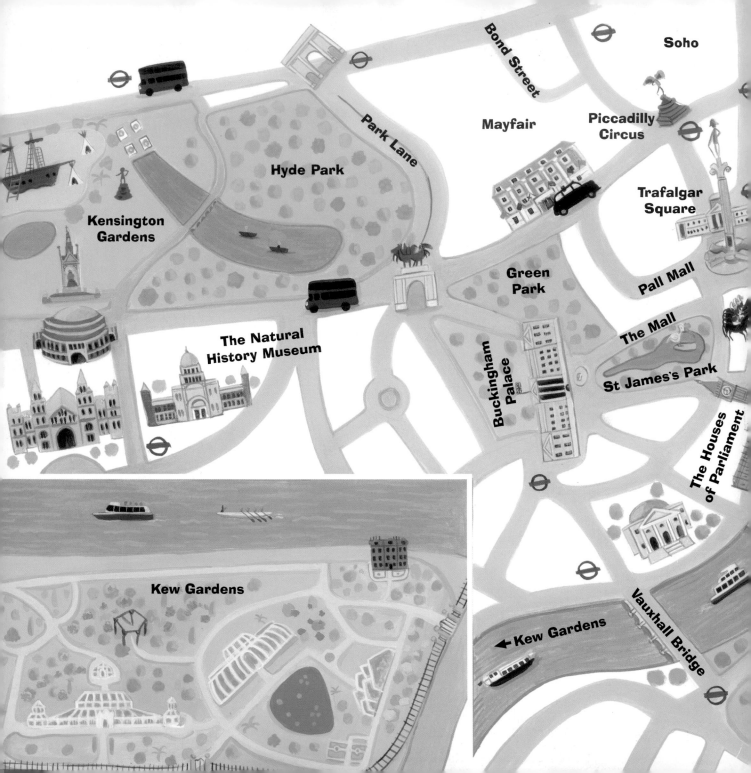